Kola Nut & 'Oney

Poetry to evoke gladness, sadness, and everything else in between.

By LeRoi Poet

A letter to... **You**,

Love. We all need it right? It comes in many different forms, bringing joy and purpose to all we do. As sweet as love is, being human beings, our lives are also riddled with times of heartbreak; one cannot exist without the other. In this book I will share the different ways these energies have passed through my soul.

This book has been a long time coming as I have been writing and sharing fragments of my being with friends and family for years through various digital platforms, but now is the right time to give you a tangible part of me, allowing you to see the world from my lens, what would you find, or who?

If you're reading this I hope you thoroughly enjoy the book and I appreciate every second you take to absorb my very essence through art. Though the book can be read in a traditional 'page to page', front to back fashion; my hope is that afterwards you will randomly open the book anywhere and either relate or feel inspired – becoming a muse itself.

Once again thank you for breathing new life into my art with your own perspective and I look forward to connecting and hearing back from you all.

God bless,
LeRoi Poet

Table of Contents

Instrumentalove

She is a golden brown all over,
Like a warm sunset.

When I place my lips,
On hers, and blow a tender kiss,
She plays a song filling me with bliss,

Her curved body entwined in my arms,
Light and overcome by calm,
She whispers in my ear:

Wish we could stay,
Still...
In this loving embrace.

Stroking down her neck,
Whilst running my fingers down her body,
Till I rub over her buttons gently,
Pushing them softly.

"Is she the reason?"

Is she the reason that I push myself?
Imagining showering her with all my wealth,
You brought me into this world and raised me into
a man,
Now it's my turn to raise you up as high as I can.
The irreplaceable, beautiful black queen,
Who showed me true beauty is felt and not seen.
Mother, you are one reason I grind,
but no money, or time given could draw us
remotely even.

Is she the reason I'm trying to be the best man I
can be?
To be the husband of the house and raise my own
family.
We speak of all these dreams and have all these
ambitions,
All these aims, now delivering on them is my only
mission.
I pledge to you my whole being, to be happy is
the goal,
As we move full steam ahead like trains full of
charcoal.

I ask myself, Is she the reason that I write?
So that when she gets older she just might,
Read poetic stories written by her big bro,

And understand this life is so much more,
Than what you see on the outside,
Rather what you feel on the inside.
Never give up sis, in all things just try,
Laugh a lot, be ambitious, alert with the mind's eye.
Understand my sisters you are the future queens,
You must aim higher than where your mothers have been,
Change begins with you, and must believe like I do in what you could do!

They're the reason I grin, smile, and left beaming,
Locked jaw, dimples, I can't keep my teeth in.
Motivated to push myself harder
And pray that my goals continue to be drawn closer

Love is like a rose

Love is like a rose,
Vibrant as the petals that grow
On its stem, so strong and divine,
Growing stronger with passing time.
Take a chance; pull it from the roots with haste
So you may experience & smell, the delicate taste.

Love is like a rose,
We don't know how many thorns we can take,
With no liquid trust, the stem deteriorates,
And like the petals, our hearts easily break.

First Dance

Baby girl close your eyes listen to the smooth beat,
Let's dance, synchronised moving of our feet
Take my hand let me show you how it goes,
Follow my lead baby, yeah nice and slow.
Move in and place your arms around my neck,
Imagine it's just you and me, no one else is on deck.
I'll rub my hands down your body resting at your waist,
Don't hesitate, you can use my chest to rest your pretty face.

How much I love her

How much do I love her? No poem could show,
I could not express in the words I say,
For today's love will mature day by day,
Engraved in my heart it will always grow

I love her with every part of my soul,
She fills me with more warmth than a sun ray,
I love her eyes, like stars twinkling away,
My affection burns slowly with red coal.

I do not feel like I have done enough!
Should I have danced a dance or sung a song?
Love makes you feel, to impress constantly.
The small things matter, it's not really tough,

I see now a poem is very strong
For my love is preserved eternally.

Midnight musings

Sometimes I watch you sleep, not hearing a breath or seeing you stir…
And I briefly panic at thoughts of losing the love of my world.

Finding Herself

High grade student, future looking bright,
Sky's the limit, soaring high like a kite,
All of a sudden, it all took a plight
Stop watching me
Judging me...
"She's fat"
"She's ugly"
This is messed up
You don't even know me.

Begun with starving herself all day,
Happy she lost a few pounds, but the wrong way.
Dinner-time, sitting with the family,
"Can I eat in my room?", she asks politely.
Her parents let her go,
She went to the toilet though,
Lifted the commode,
Forcing fingers down her throat.
In the magazines all she sees,
Are size zero idols, classed as celebrities,
Seen on posters, billboards and TV,
Manipulating you like that's what you have to be.
Days turned into weeks,
A's turned into C's,
She's now classed as "cool", no longer as "geek".
Something's not right, she's still not happy,
I asked her what's up?

And this is what she told me:

"What am I doing?
I've got a future to be pursuing.
It's not about money, fame or the latest ride,
I'm deeper than that, what counts is the inside.
I need to get back on track with my old life,
Ignore things that want to cause me strife.
Geek, Neek, Nerd whatever you call it,
In the end I know I will make it.
So you watch me
Judge me...
Call me fat Or ugly
Truth is
I'm happy
God made me
So uniquely!"

A woman

You are a woman and very beautiful,
Don't believe the negativity from any fool.
You all have your own style,
"You just have to find it, even though...
It may take a while"
Start off with respecting yourself,
Never feel like, you're below anybody else.
You are unique in your own way,
If they don't like you, for you, you don't need
them anyway!

Don't be afraid, to let out your feelings,
And stand up for what you believe in.
When times are hard, keep your head up,
Be True to yourself, you'll rise to the top.
You won't find your prince and get the best,
Unless you see yourself first as a princess.

Miss Pohitry 1.1

I've got to say thank you
For doing what you do.
I can feel your magic
Coming over me quick.
You're still my first crush
Giving me such a rush
Of words so delicately
Placed in poetry.

I can do anything with you by my side.
To my soul you constantly sing
When my eyes are shut wide.
I thank God for giving you to me,
Such a huge part of my life.
Thinking about you constantly,
My true release to all the strife.

Growing Pains

Shed so many tears,
Salt raindrops, splatter pavements,
For lost childhood peers...

Why Wait...?

Only once, you are this young,
Why wait to go out and play?
Enjoy life now, won't be too long,
Till the skies turn blue to grey.

Why wait? When your fruit has ripened,
Now it is at its most sweet,
In time its taste shall only worsen,
And I'll look for others to eat.

Should a farmer not sow his seeds
In rich and fertile land?
Why wait till it's burdened barren with weeds
And given no use by God's own hands.

So Shy It Hurts

I watch her pack her books, about to leave,
Opens the bin to throw her drink away,
My soul within is sad and wants to grieve,
Why...you ask? For the "Hi" I did not say.

She's thinking why does he not speak to me,
Truthfully I think he's really handsome,
Dropped a million hints the whole journey,
In my heart, I feel as if it's his turn.

It has to be the fear of rejection,
That restrains me back, body stays so still,
Thus filling me with such hesitation,
Forcing me to act against my own will.

I truly cannot think of what is worst,
Than being, oh so shy until it hurts.

Mother and Son

Came into the world a premature birth
Struggling in the doctors' arms to breathe
To draw that breath and expand his girth
Mums eyes closed – praying, have to believe.
With no hesitation they hurried to incubation,
Laid gently and placed wires in him, like a
playstation.
Things seem bleak not looking too good,
It's been 5minutes, hope is growing cold and stiff
as wood.
No pulse picked up by the machine,
Doctors are losing their self esteem.
But not the mother, she forces herself to her feet
Wearily approaching courageously.
"I'm here for you so don't give up on me,
The lord sent you to make history,
So wake up son, fulfil your destiny"

I will always be there for you,
In your struggles to pull you through,
There's nothing I wouldn't do – Just ask me,
I am your mother and love you unconditionally,
There'll be no need to hide,
For I will always be by your side.

Mum watches intensely out of blurred eyes,
She sees the slightest movement, he begins to softly cry
"Thank you God" she proclaims out loud
For a son that sings that beautiful sound
Wrapped in a blanket, a nice warm cover,
They pass him over to his weeping mother.

I will always be there for you,
In your struggles to pull you through,
There's nothing I wouldn't do – Just ask me,
I am your mother and love you unconditionally,
There'll be no need to hide,
For I will always be by your side.

Instantly she felt this strong link
She could feel his heart and hers beating in sync.
He opens his eyes of innocence,
To a mother with a smile so vibrant.
He copies, dimples developed and pink gums,
Mum takes out her breast to fill up his tum.
She helps him to get his first feed,
And build up the strength his body needs...

several weeks, nearly two months have passed,
Look at how he's changed, now got a firm grasp.
Eyes bright and alert, holding onto mum's finger,
Kicking out with his feet when he joins her in laughter.
The Son and Mother, growing closer forever.

The whale and the sea

I am the whale and you're the calm sea,
Constantly beside me, calm & peacefully,
Gently being caressed by your tide,
Even when weak, helping me get by,
I'm curious to experience your depths,
Discovering your inner beauty and deep intellect,
I sing to you daily, in a smooth sax voice,
Echoing I love you, till you tsunami and rejoice.

When we don't get along, you wave,
Me away, as if to pave,
A new tide, for a new whale,
To move into, I say
No way, I'm adamant to stay,
Your mine, not a baton in relay,
Promising to love you much more,
Till the waves subside and crash into the shore.

When the scorching sun and breeze dries my skin,
I find a safe sanctuary deep within
Your warm, liquid lubrication.
Going deeper, deeper, deeper,
Til I feel the growing pressure,
Squeezing my body tighter,
Then, your coral nails run down my body,
Relaxing me, to blow out bubbles slowly...

Moving her...

It involves improvisation in the conversation.
A shot of confidence to drown the hesitation.
Recite to oneself "I will make her mine",
Because her eyes are like diamonds with a lingering shine.

Anyways here I go...

Would you be my valentine?

Would you be my valentine?
Today, and say you're all mine,
Not game – real talk, no wacky lines,
The only girl, all the time, staying in mind.
I want to hold your hand out in public,
So everybody knows you're my fly chick,
I want something lasting, nothing quick,
My heart is a candle burning loves eternal wick.

I've been struck by cupid,
This feeling can't be hid,
Don't want to spend another day apart,
You're my destined counterpart.
Let's tie the knot; we're the lace,
Around you I feel out of place,
You may sit and wonder why….?
Loose butterflies make me feel shy.

Beautiful on the inside,
That's what matters most,
That's where the soul reside,
"To us" I say, we toast.
Baby we can take it slow,
There's no need to rush,
I Love you more than you know.

Signed…
Your Secret Crush

Kisses with the misses - A '6 second prompt'

It happened 6 seconds from now,
5... Subtle steps towards each other,
4... By 4 fingers, intertwined,
3... Soul felt words spoken,
2... Pair of eyes closing in sync,
1... Sharp breath of anticipation...
....
Infinite butterflies

"Yum Yum"

I place my lips upon her sugary skin,
Tongue rests, gently stroking,
whilst I sink canine teeth slowly in,

Her soft flesh trembles then gives way,
Cracking crystals moan "Eat me like a buffet"

Instrumentalove #2

She is a deep ebony, I could almost taste,
A luxurious tone of dark choco-late.

Each of the 88 keys she holds,
Unlocks a door for my passion to unfold.
I call out to her "hey boo",
She opens up, "I love you!"
I smile feeling the same way too,
Because no one understands me like you do.

Relax deeply, I'll massage your temples to the left,
Lost in your chords... Calmness settles, perfect.

My feet pass over your ankles,
Your spine shivers with prolonged thrills;
Each pulse is warm and subtle

And, whenever I rub the inside of your right thigh...
You give me chills...
As your moan hits them lofty highs,

Passing thoughts

I can be your hubby like a good sport...

"I fell in love" #1

I fell in love and I don't think I've gotten up yet,
I close my eyes and relive the days of when we first met.
All was right and the future looked perfect,
The moons warm glow led to dreaming of you at night,
And how beautiful you were in my sight.
Until I awoke to the beaming cold sun,
And my daymare has once again begun,
Because you are no longer with me, long gone.

Am I to love like this again?

When I look in her eyes they twinkle like
constellations of the night sky,
Her skin is clear and smooth as dairy milk silk.
I dream of tasting her liquorice lips,
The sweet kind that leaves you reminiscing,
Wishing for just one more kiss.
She soothes my soul with a voice like harps played
in heaven,
Blissful when in her presence, scent sweeter than
vanilla incense.

Engulfed in warm and pure love,
Am I to love someone like this again?
Sweet and innocent love,
Am I to be loved like this again?

"I fell in love" #2

I fell in love, by no means a cruise,

I'm slowly getting up, but my heart bears the bruise.

Listening daily to Maxwell's Pretty Wings,

In my heart dwells an empty feeling,

Because, I know it's her I'm missing,

All I think of is picking up the phone to call,

But I keep hitting a doubts wall,

Just once I say, just to hear her voice,

But sadly in reality, that wouldn't be the right choice.

What's that saying? Time is a healer?,

But I don't think any amount of time will stop me thinking of her.

Heartbreak

Heartbreak, Heartbreak, Heartbreak!
One of those feelings that make,
Your heart weak with every thump
And leaves in your throat a lingering lump,
Making one hug their pillow whilst they dream;
Thinking it's her. Before waking and it isn't what it seems.

Regrets

Sitting here, thinking of my boo,

Damn... what am I going to do?

Sorry, for how I hurt you in the past,

But I'm begging you baby girl, give me another chance.

Rain reminds me of the tears that you shed,

Like the weather your feelings I sometimes misread,

Now I'm alone in bed – Wishing I saw back then way ahead,

The conflicts of my heart and my head.

I fell in love #3

I fell in love, now it's time to move on,
I still love her, but not in love with the same
passion,
Through faint smiles, blurry eyes and fallen tears,
I'm deleting and cutting up times that we shared.

Slowly, but surely I'm starting to let go,
Of things not going to happen no more.
Freedom - I wish her the very best,
Now my heart can heal and finally rest.

Instrumentalove #3

Strumming her A string, B string, then
the spot, where her G string should've been...

"I fell in love" #4

I fell in love and I have no regrets,
I see now, love is just another of life's tests.
I pray, Lord you choose the right lady for me,
I know she's out there, my wife to be.
I'm willing to wait however
Long your fate takes to bring us together.

I fell in love and honestly, I have no regrets,
Because now I think I know what it takes to make
love perfect.

Superman

They said they wanted superman, well I know just the man.
Comforting and wisdom giving to help you understand,
Anything on your mind, just rely on him,
And he will share his light on your life looking dim,
Like a flare burning bright in pitch darkness,
Leading you and providing great guidance,
Forgiveness & Unconditional kindness.
With your heart, be willing to take his hand,
He will then slowly but surely, reveal his plans,
There's a life he has that we don't even know yet,
Prove that you want it and he will never forget,
To fulfil all your hearts dreams,
There's much more to this life than it seems,
He knows where you've been and determined where you're going,
And will aid your spirit inl growing

He has no weaknesses to kryptonite,
Holds power to change hearts of bloods and crips tonight
There is no mountain he cannot move,
All he wants is to show you his love and shine through you,
Always present, there's no need to fear,

Even when in the deepest pit he will show he cares.
Helping you until you're free,
Making the impossible, possible for you to see.
If you need this superman just glorify his name,
Then he begins working, you won't even know he came,
Till positivity swings your way then all you can say is
Superman is here and here he is to stay.
Makes you want to grab that mic and get up on stage,
And hope the world is listening while you proclaim:

I'm talking about a superman
The true superman
His work is pretty, pretty super man!
His presence leaves me feeling quite super man!
In his dictionary there's no word like can't.

I'm talking about a superman
The only superman
So amazing, my superman!
His presence leaves me feeling quite super man!
In his dictionary there's no word like can't.

A song for her #2

Sorry, excuse me miss, I don't mean to bother you,
(She stops... my heart double-dutches, why is she so beautiful?)
Your eyes had me mesmerized from across the street,
And your dimples made me weak when you smiled, you look so sweet.
I'm digging your style like an artefact,
You must be single, because you are in fact,
My soul mate, so let's pursue and not wait,
Or regret on what could have been
a fairy-tale future, starring you and me.

Tropical Summers

Shall I compare her to a summer's day?
Well if I'm being realistic then I'll say:
The love in our hearts burn like incense,
Driving away bad omens, wanting to pose as
friends,

We're more like amazon tropical storms,
Hot heads combined with cool hearts clashing,
But how'd you stay mad at the one you adore?
Apologetic... making up til dawn, with thunderous
passion...

Bitter-Sweet

Dear God,

I hope that my sinful ways, don't lead me too far astray,

Ending up a young dad mingling with these lustful babes.

Praying for focus, fighting these inner demons, which eat up my spirit like locusts.

They prey on my weakness, playing with my biological instincts:

To leave them twisted - Raw, not thinking of repercussions,

Lying to parents, to get my ego rubbed around town,

"I've got footy," When I know deep down

I really should be:

At home studying for these GCSE exams,

Instead of helping this girl get over her Ex Sam,

Damn...

PSA

All we hear is men don't cry, you have to be strong. The stereotype that prevails is that we as men when confronted with problems should just "SuCk It Up" and handle it. What makes this even crazier is when you take into consideration that the suicide rate amongst men is higher compared to women pretty much globally. The coping mechanisms for boys and eventually men are obviously not working.

Honestly, this is why I am eternally grateful I have been blessed with the ability to share my thoughts and emotions through my poetry. We are human beings capable of feeling emotions on all points of the spectrum from gladness to sadness. When those inevitable periods of sadness or doom and gloom are upon us I want you to know you're not alone, what you're feeling is valid and there is a purpose for you in tomorrow.

Shall we continue?

Nostalgic Nuggets

Then he woke up one day and he didn't feel the longing in his heart anymore.

He reflected on time. Time is a funny old thing; healing and growth is it's partner, and all three are constantly working with each other to the betterment of you.

Past relationships became one of those smells in the air that elicit vivid memories, nostalgic nuggets of time, if you like.

No limits

I really can not wait to get my piano.
I know, there is another side of me to show,
I feel the creativity in my blood flow,
Pulsing through my interior, looking for places to go,
Places to grow, places to fully express,

Seeking adventures in places I do not know, And i must confess,
That I find it all very exciting, the thought leaves my body tingling
Causing cherubs to start singing.
Leroi Poet: A writer, spoken word artist, a creator, hopefully one day a pianist,
The latter will take time, but I'm committed to this.

How do i...?

How do I tell loved ones, I've fought suicidal thoughts?

And sometimes when I close my eyes, demons try to haunt

Me, with what-ifs, anxiety and danger,

Falling from cliffs, pills til I OD, home invaded by strangers,

Feeling low, drained on some days, like what really is the point?

Tempted to join bros in lighting up indigo joints,

I've never been fond, but heard, that the herb, relieves the stress,

But when the high leaves, gravity WILL bring you down to the same earthly mess?

The wind…

The wind strokes my face,
Cool, across hair follicles,
Refreshing and calm...

Venice sunsets

The sky is like a ripened peach with mellow tones
of pink and yellows.
Birds heading to nests sing sweetly, flying freely
into sunsets.

There's a slight scent of the sea lingering in the air.
Coupled with a gentle breeze dancing in
between hairs.

I close my eyes, finding comfort in my silence,
Finally feeling free in beautiful Venice.

Toasting GOATs in the flesh

For a moment, I want you to forget all your other musical tastes,
Acknowledge Nasir as the legend he is while he breathes with us today.

Mustard seed

Believe in the king in me and I'll never let you go,
Never let you fall, keep you in close proximity to my soul.
If you believe in the king in me, I will in time, show
There's nothing to fear be it in the past, present or countless tomorrows.

I love her

I love her, I tell her every day,
Because you don't lose by giving
Only when you refrain...

Musicspiration...

Nas fuqs with my mind, Tupac with my soul,
Even though the former is still here, the onus is on
Kendrick and J Cole.

Dear unborn son…

I'm trying to carve out of my soul, the man I want you to aspire to be,
Ambitious, self confident, void of insecurities.
You are my prince and love comes from within,
Love your strengths and your flaws, nobody's perfect - we are all destined to sin.
You will face many hardships, that's one factual life characteristic,
But I believe in you to overcome all... breathe, regroup and handle your business.
Never lose sight of the Crown I've bestowed upon your heart
You will be great. God blessed, handsome and set apart,
From all those around you, the head and never the tail,
And in all stormy waters, your spirit will always sail...

Love you.

Brunch?

Goodmorning, excuse me Miss, would you mind slowing down?

I've noticed you wandering this specific part of town,

In the mornings buying milk, hair bubbled in a ponytail,

You make my heart tick, I've got to get your name without fail,

Don't look away, because you're out without the superficial make up,

Your vibe captivates me, to unearth the tangible make up,

Of the atoms found within your soul,

So can I get your number, and let's discover how the next chapter unfolds...

Fireplace

Nubian Queen, take a nibble on my lips,
I crave your sensuality, all I ask for is this.

But wait!

Let's first explore how our mind fits,
intensifying the lustful desire,
Before divulging on the wood between these hips,
To throw on your hungry fire.

Miss Pohitry deux

No matter the weather, I can count on J Dilla,
To soothe my mind, he will never dither,
Disappoint, thus letting me down,
In a gloomy and glum winter in London town,
Instrumentals relax my inner being you see?
I become subdued with tranquillity.

Honestly, believe it or not, I leave this world,
Spiritually; to a place where Miss Pohitry can be
heard,
Whispering gently, her voice massages my
temples,
I resemble a mortar, Miss Pohitry the Pestle,
Grinding wisdom into my muscles
With intent, in small circles.

MmMm...

Yeah... Miss P.
Work on me...
hmm... Right there...
Fingers entwined in her Afro hair.

I want [An affirmation of Love]

I want a woman that inspires me to be more than I think I can be,
A woman who wants to build an empire, a visionary.

Until I meet her, I'm going to live a life full of love and progress,
Overcoming struggles, praying to stay God blessed.
Harnessing the energy, from lessons set before me,
Ultimately aiming and growing to be...

The man that inspires her to be more than she thinks she can be,
Her lover, best friend, guardian of her mind, body and spirituality.

Telescopic Arousal

As a young boy I wanted a telescope,
To peer at jewels blanketing the night skies.

Now as a man I cannot cope,
With the gyrating galaxies within her eyes.

Dear Lisboa,

I came to you for a rest and you gave it to me,
You supplied fresh seafood when I was hungry
and satisfied my sweet tooth with your pastries,
Allowed me to explore the vein like roads of your
body,
Going deep in your caves, falling in love so
deeply,
I relaxed in gardens, with your subtle sweet sea
scent in the air,
As light breezes whispered latin in both of my ears.
You provided company, so I will not be alone,
People radiating warmth and laughter working my
jaw bone,
We looked out at the ocean, lost in the moments
between waves,
Of all the women, Lisboa you're one of my faves,
You shared scars, the physical and the mental,
Showed how you overcame adversity, becoming
more beautiful.

Lisboa, I will return, you I will never forget

With love, and till next time, Beijinhos,
LeRoi Poet

Savannahs hunger

Muphasa belly
Roars violently when hungry,
Food glorious food...

"You're being weak…"

Previous relationships left me with bulging baggage,

Opting to temporarily stay single, and not pass on the damage.

That damage, I've acknowledged your eerie existence,

But I will not be beaten; spiritually laced with a Godly Resistance,

A persistence, to love and fulfil my potential,

Putting my all into everything is one of my main credentials...

Credentials? Specific aspects that define my character,

The next challenge is how I react to the end of this chapter...

New beginnings

You know guys this life is so crazy. So, I've been dating this lady and lately,

I've been thinking maybe just maybe... I'm 100% sure actually..

She's the one to sway me, from the single life of meaningless dirty dancing, word to Patrick Swayze.

We lay in the sheets swooning in each other's company, celestial banter; you could say heavenly, it just feels meant for me, she treats me good, I feel understood, as I reciprocate that soul therapy.

"You're being weak, but..."

Can you know love, without experiencing hate?
Will you appreciate peace without chaos?
For countless days, I struggled to concentrate,
When each scenario seemed to result in a loss,
A loss? Usually the prerequisite for a win!
My answer wasn't external but found within.
Within! I came face to face with a raging soul,
looking at these pieces, which were once whole...

"You're being weak, but I've also felt your strength..."

From this day forward, you will drop the self-destruction. See the good in all things?, Hmph! See things for what they are - Good or bad. This experience was a necessary one, brother. As cliche as it sounds. What doesn't kill you, will only make you stronger. So you get up, back on your path to greatness, back on your spiritual walk, get your career, physical and mental health all back in line. You're being weak, but I've also felt your strength, I've felt its depths and I know you're waking up.

Now go and be great.

Le FIN.

In this world, we just want to belong, Ultimately finding peace in a place or with someone.
I challenge you to find that piece within someone special, someone who makes all things fall into place perfectly, bringing clarity and purpose to your personal journey. Look into a mirror and peer into that person's eyes right now, tell them:

- In the end, I will be great
- There will be setbacks, but I will rise
- Good things are coming my way
- I am loved and worthy to be loved

Thank you all for being a part of my journey and I pray to God you will find your own peace in this world, until we meet again...

Be You. Be Beautiful.
LeRoi Poet

Thank you for taking the time to finish my first poetry collection book. More books are in the works from poetry to self-help. It would be great and help me massively if you could:

- Leave a review on Amazon, which would improve my discoverability to others
- Connect with me on Instagram, search **Leroipoet.** I'd love to hear your thoughts.

Til Next Time

<3

Printed in Great Britain
by Amazon